MY MOMMY IS A NURSE PRACTITIONER

Written by
Kim Harkness

Illustrated by
Patricia Grace Claro

 FriesenPress

One Printers Way
Altona, MB R0G 0B0
Canada

www.friesenpress.com

ISBN
978-1-03-830583-1 (Hardcover)
978-1-03-830582-4 (Paperback)
978-1-03-830584-8 (eBook)

1. JUVENILE NONFICTION, CAREERS

Distributed to the trade by The Ingram Book Company

Dedicated to my Boyzos:
Alan, Aidan, Liam, and Winston

MY MOMMY
IS A NURSE PRACTITIONER.

What exactly is

a NURSE PRACTITIONER?

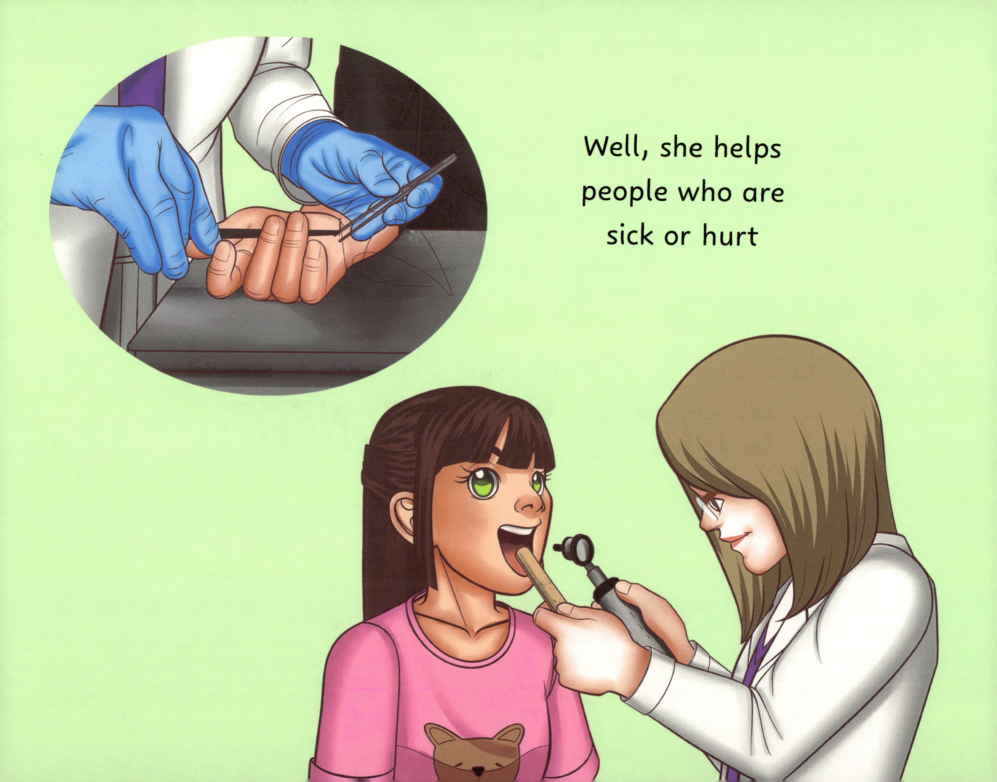

Well, she helps people who are sick or hurt

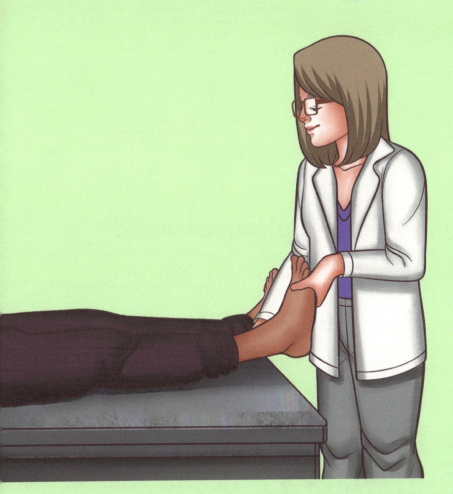

or who want to stay
healthy for a long,
long time.

She looks people over head to toe, she tells them what is making them sick,

and she chooses the right medicine for them.

Wait a minute . . .

IS MY MOMMY A DOCTOR?

She says that doctors and NURSE PRACTITIONERS sometimes do similar things, but they are different. When they are learning how to do their jobs, they go to different schools and practice in different ways.

Sometimes **MOMMY** works with doctors and sometimes she does not.

Sometimes she sends people to doctors called "specialists" to test their bodies, find out what is making them sick, and help them get better.

She gets to work with a lot of different people with really cool jobs!

MOMMY used to work as a nurse! Then she went back to school to become a **NURSE PRACTITIONER**.

(Mommy was in school for a **LOOOOONG** time.)

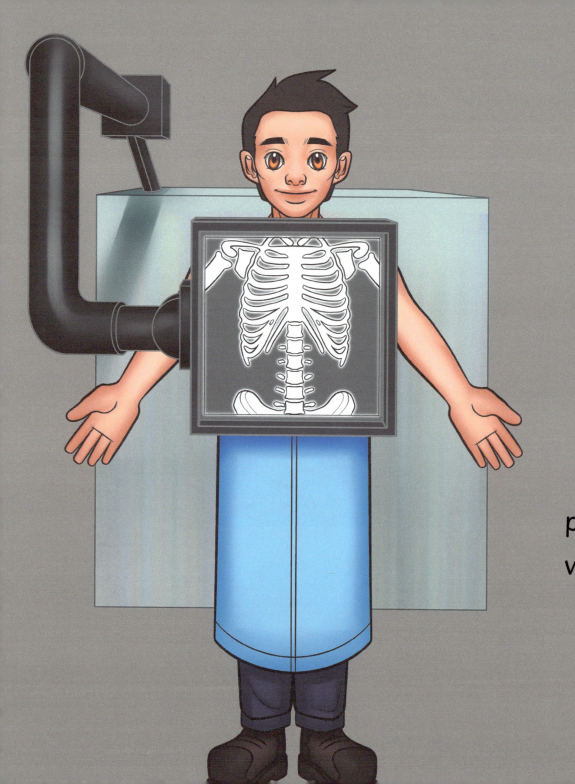

She is different from other nurses because she can do special things that only doctors and **NURSE PRACTITIONERS** can do, like sending people to get pictures of their insides and writing orders for medicine.

MOMMY says there aren't very many Nurse Practitioners, and we need more of them to help people when they are sick.

* 2.5% of all nurses in Ontario are Nurse Practitioners

Some days **MOMMY** comes home tired and some days she even comes home sad. Most days Mommy's job is hard, but some days it's really, really hard.

She tells me my hugs help cheer her up and that
they are the best medicine there is.

What makes MY MOMMY

a GOOD NURSE PRACTITIONER?

Well, she's very creative, she is always kind, and she is really, really smart!

MN

Hon. BSc

Hon. BScN

NP-Led Clinic

She says she loves her job because she gets to help a lot of people.

Maybe one day I'll be

a NURSe PRaCTiTiONeR Too!

But the best part about **MOMMY** being
a **NURSE PRACTITIONER** is . . .

SHE FINDS LOTS OF TIME TO SPEND WITH ME.

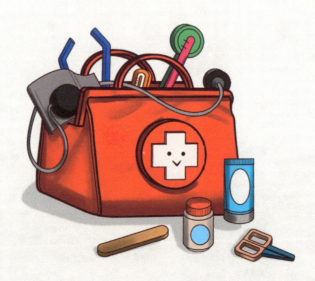

ABOUT THE AUTHOR

Kim Harkness is a Nurse Practitioner at a community hospital in the Greater Toronto Area. She is also an Adjunct Lecturer at the Lawrence S. Bloomberg Faculty of Nursing at the University of Toronto, as well as a longstanding member of the Nurse Practitioners' Association of Ontario. As a health and wellness advocate, Kim provides quality and compassionate care to her community. This is her first book which marries her professional passion with her dream of being an author of a children's book.

Kim's pride and joy are her two little boys whose endless curiosity and creativity amaze her. When she isn't taking care of patients Kim enjoys crocheting, watching true crime, walking her dog and, most importantly, spending time with her family.

Printed in the USA
CPSIA information can be obtained
at www.ICGtesting.com
JSHW041235240824

68563JS00008B/4